THIS DIARY BELONGS TO

Lauren

$5.99

PONY CAMP diaries

Lauren and Lucky

For Tom, with huge thanks for all
your wonderful work on Pony Camp xx

tiger tales

5 River Road, Suite 128, Wilton, CT 06897
Published in the United States 2020
Originally published in Great Britain in 2007
by the Little Tiger Group
Text copyright © 2007, 2020 Kelly McKain
Illustrations copyright © 2007, 2020 Mandy Stanley
ISBN-13: 978-1-68010-453-0
ISBN-10: 1-68010-453-5
Printed in China
STP/1800/0294/1019
All rights reserved
10 9 8 7 6 5 4 3 2 1

For more insight and activities, visit us at www.tigertalesbooks.com

PONY CAMP diaries

Lauren and Lucky

by Kelly McKain

Illustrated by Mandy Stanley

tiger tales

Other titles in the series:

Contents

Dear Riders,

A warm welcome to Sunnyside Stables!

Sunnyside is our home, and for the next week it will be yours, too! We're a big family—my husband, Jason, and I have two children, Olivia and Tyler, plus two dogs ... and all the ponies, of course!

We have friendly yard staff and a very talented instructor, Sally, to help you get the most out of your week. If you have any worries or questions about anything at all, just ask. We're here to help, and we want your vacation to be as enjoyable as possible—so don't be shy!

As you know, you will have a pony to take care of as your own for the week. Your pony can't wait to meet you and start having fun! During your stay, you'll be caring for your pony, improving your riding, enjoying long rides in the country, learning new skills, and making new friends.

And this week's special activity is a trip to the All-County Show, where you'll see some fabulous dressage and so many exciting displays! Add swimming, games, movies, barbecues, and a gymkhana, and you're in for a fun-filled vacation to remember!

This special Pony Camp Diary is for you to fill with your vacation memories. We hope you'll write all about your adventures here at Sunnyside Stables—because we know you're going to have a lot of them!

Wishing you a wonderful time with us!

Jess xx

Monday lunchtime—
here I am at Pony Camp!

Us girls are sitting on the benches outside
the farmhouse in the sunshine, and we've all
decided to start our diaries at the same time!
It's been fantastic here so far—I've met all
these awesome girls, been given a fantastic
pony, and we've had our first riding lesson.
Wow! I've just realized that I've got a ton to
say, so I'll try writing really quickly!

By the time Mom and I got here, most
of the other girls had already arrived and
unpacked their stuff. Mom had to rush right off
again 'cos she'd left my three brothers in the
car, so Jess (who runs Pony Camp) showed
me up to my room. All the way up the stairs
I was babbling on about how I'd chosen to
come this week because there's a chance to do
dressage. I've done a few tests at shows near

13

where I live on Fizz or Gregory, the ponies I ride at my local stables, and I'm really excited about learning more. And it's great 'cos some of the girls here are as dressage-crazy as me! My horsey friends back home are crazy about showjumping instead, so I don't usually get to talk about dressage that much.

When Jess and I got up to the room, the top bunk was already taken by a girl named Arabella, so I took the bottom one. The messy bed by the window turned out to be Jess's daughter Olivia's. She's really nice—in fact, everyone here is.

After we'd said our names, Arabella was like, "Well, the girls in the oldest room all came together, and Olivia will be riding in the

YOU'LL HAVE TO BE MY FRIEND!

other group 'cos she's not into dressage, so *you'll* have to be my friend." I couldn't figure out if she was joking or not, but she just smiled and put her arm

through mine, and we
went down to the
yard together. That's
where we met the
other girls, and we
were all saying hi and
telling each other what
riding we've done
and that kind of
thing.

After Sally showed us around the yard and
gave us a safety talk, it was time to meet our
ponies. We all stood in the yard feeling really
excited as Lydia the stable girl brought them
out one by one and helped us mount up. Sally
said usually we would have an assessment
lesson to figure out which groups we'll be in,
but this week we don't need one 'cos there'll
just be a dressage group and a normal group.

The dressage group (Group B) is:

Paula, age 12, who's Spanish, with **Flame**.

Leona, also 12, who's German and is Paula's best friend, with **Charm**.

Marie, Leona's younger sister, who's 10 like me, with **Mischief**.

Arabella, also 10, with **Gracie**, her own pony (who's a sweet Arab mare with a cute snip on her nose)—how lucky is that!

♫ Lauren and Lucky ♫

Me, **Lauren**, and (drum roll, please!) the most gorgeous, cutest pony I have ever seen, my handsome **LUCKY**!

I couldn't believe my luck when Sally said he was for me. My LUCK in getting LUCKY—hee-hee! He's beautiful—a 10-year-old 14hh blue roan cob with a cascading flowing mane, cute clumpy feet, and the most beautiful eyes.

Arabella said, "Lauren, don't you think he's a little too heavy for dressage?" But I just pointed out how well Charlotte Dujardin did on Valegro, who's a heavier build, before he retired. And the crowd absolutely LOVED him. Arabella looked a little surprised and muttered, "Fair point."

I gave Lucky an extra pat, just in case he knew she wasn't being very nice about him.

As I said, Olivia is riding with Group A, 'cos she figures her pony, Tally, doesn't exactly get the concept of dressage and is only really happy when he's dragging her through a hedge!

The others in Group A are:

Polly, who is 8, riding **Jewel**.

Bea, who's also 8, on spirited **Cookie**.

And **Jojo**, only just 7, on **Sugar**.

Lauren and Lucky

Sally

Jess

Sally taught our group, and Jess taught
Group A. We were nervous and excited as we
mounted up and made our way to the manège.
But we didn't suddenly start doing really hard
dressage movements or anything—it was just a
normal lesson for Sally to see what we can do.

It was wonderful riding Lucky. He's really
chilled out, which is great, but he's not exactly
quick off the leg! I'll have to get him to perk
up for the dressage test, somehow.

While we were walking around on a long
rein to cool down, Sally told us she's got a
surprise in store, but she's not going to reveal
it until this afternoon. Of course, we were
all begging her to tell us right away, but she
just did a zipping her lips sign and looked
mysterious.

When the lesson finished, we all dismounted and ran up our stirrups, and Sally asked Leona to lead the way back to the barn to untack. Then when we reached the yard, Arabella tried to hand Gracie's reins to Lydia.

Lydia laughed and said, "Nice try, but we all take care of our own ponies here. That's the point!"

Arabella laughed, too, and said, "'Course. Only joking!" But I didn't really know if she was or not. How strange! I'd be desperate to do everything I could for my pony if I had one. Especially if it was my handsome Lucky! I'd do anything for *him*!

Lucky was so funny in the barn. Like when I was grooming him, he kept turning his head and trying to eat the body brush. He also nudged the tack box over with his nose—to see if there were any treats at the bottom, probably! I love him so much already, and when I gave him a big pat and rubbed his head, he gave a happy snort and nuzzled into my shoulder, so I think he loves me, too.

Arabella was waiting by the barn door for me so we could go in for lunch together, but I had to keep popping back to see Lucky! She just stood there, going, "Hurry up, I'm hungry!" so I gave him one last hug, and then I gave Gracie one, too, so she didn't feel left out.

For lunch we had chicken and salad and—

Oh, we're all off to the yard now. Sally's going to reveal her surprise! Well, fast writing worked, 'cos I got down almost everything we've done so far!

What a great surprise!

We're about to have our workshop, and I'm just quickly scribbling this while Sally went to find the markers for the whiteboard. The surprise is:

We're going to create our own dressage tests, set to MUSIC!

I know from watching the Winter Dressage Championships on *Horse and Country TV* that this is called freestyle. It's my fave type of dressage, and it's so cool to see the horses moving in time to the music. We even get to pick what movements we want to do and choose our own tunes, too! It'll be just like doing dance routines, but on our ponies!

Well, *obviously* everyone was really excited about it and instantly started chatting about what music they might pick. Arabella did get a little worried that we wouldn't be doing

22

"proper" dressage tests like the official ones
at comps, but Sally promised her that we'll be
taking the technical side very seriously, and the
movements will have to be absolutely perfect.
Plus, there are going to be some things in
it we all have to do (called the compulsory
movements) so she can compare us more
easily. We were *all* a little nervous, but Sally
said not to worry as we'll build up our routines
step by step. Phew!

Marie had the idea of doing the comp in
fancy dress then and started saying how she
wanted to do Mischief up as a pop star and
dye his mane with different hair colorings
and put purple legwarmers
on him!

We all laughed when
Sally said, "I don't think
Mischief would be too happy
about that since he's a boy!"

But she did agree that some kind of themed dress to go with our music might be fun.

Arabella said she's just bought a brand-new regulation dressage competition jacket and jodhs and she's wearing *them*, so there! Sally smiled and said that's fine, too.

Even more exciting, when we have our trip out to the County Show on Wednesday, Sally says we'll be seeing some freestyle dressage set to music in one of the show rings. So we'll be able to get some tips from the pros, too!

Oh, she's back, gotta go....

After dinner

We're all going swimming soon, but Jess says
we have to wait a half hour first because we just
finished eating. Hopefully that's enough time to
write about what happened this afternoon!

When Sally came back, we started off
talking about the most important elements
of dressage, and she wrote a list of things like
rhythm and balance and expression, and also
that "the aim is to get yourself and your pony
moving as one, in harmony."

I figure me and Lucky
can manage that—we're
such a good team already!

Then Sally explained the compulsory
movements. She said we could work them into
our own routines however we wanted, but
that it's a good idea to make everything flowing
and symmetrical (i.e., to do each thing twice,

once on each rein). She said this is also a good idea because if you don't get something right on one rein, you still have another chance to show the judges you can do it—clever, huh?

Here's the list of compulsory movements:

Medium walk

Working trot (and also show a few lengthened strides)

20 meter circle

Working canter

Rein back 4 steps (tricky!)

We can also add other stuff like 10 meter circles, turns, all the other transitions (well, maybe not halt to canter, or even walk to canter, not for me, anyway!), serpentines, and free walk on a long rein. Leona wants to do counter-canter in hers, which is mega-difficult! Sally says it's a possibility, and we'll see how things are going. With so much choice of what to do, our routines are going to be really different from each other's!

WOW !

When it was time for our lesson, we were already totally excited, and we'd all started having ideas about what we might put in our routines. We were still chatting away as we warmed up in the manège and Sally had to tell us to calm down and concentrate! As we were walking and trotting around on each rein, she explained that one of the cornerstones of dressage is getting good impulsion, which means, well, not *speed* exactly, but more like

power through the pony's hindquarters. I don't
know exactly how to explain it, but I do know
that Lucky and I didn't have much of it! He
did wake up a little when we did a bunch of
turns, circles, half halts, and transitions, though.
Sally said he's much more expressive in his
movements when I get him going just that extra
bit more, so if I can improve his impulsion,
I should have expression figured out, too.

Flame has no problem being
expressive—she's as much of
a drama queen as Paula is,
and they look great together!

Drama Queens

Their work was amazing from the start—
and even during the warm-up, they were
sailing around in this beautiful springy trot like
complete pros. Marie's working trot looked
nice and even, too—once she'd gotten Mischief
actually on the track, that is! And Leona seems
to be able to get Charm to halt square at the

marker, never leaving a leg behind. I wish me
and Lucky could do that!

When we practiced the
compulsory movements one by
one, I found the working trot
very tricky, and Lucky didn't
at all get what I was asking
for in the rein back.

But can you believe it—
Arabella said she thought it was all easy-peasy!
Sally smiled and said, "Well, of course you can
easily do each thing on its *own*, but it's putting
the movements together and hitting specific
markers that's much more challenging."

Unlike Charm, Lucky doesn't seem that
interested in making transitions exactly at the
right markers, and that's something I really
need to work on—well, something *else*! I don't
mind, though, because there's plenty of time to
improve on everything. And I love how

relaxed Lucky is; it's part of his character, and I wouldn't want him to be any different!

I kind of wish Arabella would chill out a little, though. I don't think she *was* joking when she said I'd *have* to be her friend. She sticks to me like glue and doesn't have much to say to the other girls.

I don't mind, well, not *really* really, but it is a little annoying when I'm talking to Marie or Olivia and she just comes up and drags me off. Also, she can be a little mean about people. Like when we were untacking, she was going, "Can you believe Marie suggested hair coloring and legwarmers for Mischief? How ridiculous!"

I felt really awkward 'cos she wasn't exactly saying it very quietly and I thought Marie might hear (she was only in the next pen with Leona and their ponies). I hate it when girls gossip about each other—I just don't see the point.

So I said, "She was only excited."

Arabella got upset with me then out of nowhere and went, "Huh! Whose side are you *on?*"

So I got annoyed back and said, "I don't think there are *sides.*"

She just gave me a huffy look and began putting everything back in her tack box. That's when I realized she hadn't picked out Gracie's feet. I didn't feel like saying anything, seeing as she was being so moody with me, but on the other hand, I didn't want Gracie to have a wood chip or a stone stuck in her foot for the rest of the day. When I mentioned it, Arabella went, "I was going to do it now, *actually,*" in this really annoyed way. I don't know why she was so prickly about it. We all forget things now and then. It's no big deal.

Oh, well, never mind. I've got other things to think about—like the dressage! At dinner Leona and Paula were talking about *lateral flexion* and I was like, oh, help!

When I said how me and Lucky will be lucky to even get around, never mind anything fancy, they were really sweet and started going, "Oh, I know how you feel, I'm so awful," and "Don't worry, I'll never make it through a whole routine," even though they are AWESOME. How nice is that?! My brothers would just say, "Yeah, you're horrible!"

I wanted to sit and talk to them for longer, but Arabella dragged me off to look at her makeup collection.

Oh, gotta go—it's time to head over to the pool!

Tuesday, after lunch-
I'm just writing in here while Leona
and Paula are washing dishes ('cos
it's their turn in the rotation)

Swimming was fun last night—we all played
water games and had comps together as a
big group. Me and Arabella had such a cool
time after lights out, too. Just as I was falling
asleep, she shook my arm and suggested a
midnight snack. I wanted to wake Olivia, too,
but Arabella said she only had two lollipops
to dip in the sugar. So I climbed up onto her
bunk and we scarfed her secret stash of candy

and chatted, but in
whispers so that Jess
didn't hear us.

She was telling me
about the amazing posh
boarding school she

goes to—she keeps Gracie in the stables there, and she can ride her every single day. Imagine living at a boarding school with your pony! And think of the midnight snacks and the fun you'd have with the other girls. It must be like being at Pony Camp *all the time*! Honestly, her life sounds fabulous! And she's going on a bunch of different vacations, doing everything from drama to learning French actually in France. *And* she says her parents let her do whatever she wants, 'cos they live in Hong Kong and she only has to see them, like, twice a year or something.

So anyway, when she said all that, there I was, staring with my mouth open. "Wow, you are so, so, *so* lucky, you are lucky times one million!" I said.

"*My* dad's really strict, and my school friends live miles away so I'm stuck with my three yucky brothers most of the time. And somehow, they always seem to

wriggle out of their chores, but Mom never lets *me* off. If it wasn't for my riding lesson on Saturday mornings, I'd go crazy! I wish I could be you and always have girls to hang around with, and my own pony to ride and spend time with whenever I wanted to—it sounds like heaven to me!"

When I said all this to Arabella, she just shrugged and said, "Yeah, I guess so." She didn't seem that enthusiastic, but I know she was only playing it down so as not to rub it in. We fell asleep soon after that, so we didn't talk about it anymore.

Normally I hate getting up in the morning, but it was awesome this morning 'cos it was the first day of waking up at Pony Camp.

After breakfast, we grabbed some lead ropes from the tack room and went right off up the road to the upper field to bring in our ponies. I went up to Lucky and gave him a pat and a carrot, and he let me clip him on right away. I also helped Bea get her lead rope on Cookie because the clip was very stiff, and he kept moving his head around, the silly boy! Gracie was being a bit flighty and kept running away from Arabella, so she asked Lydia to catch her instead.

It was so nice all clip-clopping back down the road with our ponies and grooming them in the barn together, all chatting and joking— just how I'd imagined Pony Camp would be!

For our dressage workshop, our group sat at the picnic benches outside the barn. The second Sally appeared, we started bombarding her with ideas for our routines and asking questions about the compulsory movements.

"Hang on! Hang on!" she cried. "I'm glad you're excited, but one at a time!"

So we shot our hands up like we were at school and got into fits of giggles about that. Once she'd answered our questions, Sally explained that most people find it  easiest to make up the routine first and then choose music to go with it. You can have two or three different tunes put together or stick to just one if it fits well. She gave us some really good advice, which is to think about our ponies' personalities and choose the movements that suit their strengths rather than the ones that highlight their weaknesses (so me and Lucky won't be doing any halt to canter transitions, then!).

Then Sally sent Leona
to the game room to
get some rulers and
pencils and paper, and
we all copied her scale
drawing of the arena
off the whiteboard,
like this ──────→

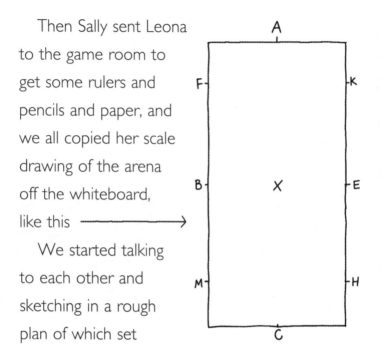

We started talking
to each other and
sketching in a rough
plan of which set
movements we could do and the best order
to do them in. There was a lot of erasing, too,
when we realized that you can't link certain ones
up very easily! There weren't enough erasers
to go around, so Arabella broke hers in half
and shared with me. We had this good idea of
doing a 20 meter circle in trot in the AX half of
the school so that when we've done the circle,

we can go into canter in the AF corner and it should look really cool. Sally came and leaned over us and said she liked that idea, and we felt really happy with ourselves!

In our lesson this morning, we worked without stirrups so we could improve our balance for the dressage. Mischief took a big plunge when he went into canter and Marie almost went out the side door, but she managed to grab the pommel in time!

We worked on the set movements again, and I think Lucky and I are actually improving. We had a turn at the 20 meter circle in trot and then at getting canter in the AF corner, the sequence Arabella and I had thought up. It worked really well, so we're definitely putting it in our routines! We also tried out trotting down the center line, then doing medium walk from C to E, then going back into trot at E. Sally's right—it is tricky when you start putting things together and trying to hit the markers.

I also remembered what she'd said about Lucky needing preparation, so I sat up tall and gave him a few extra squeezes with my legs to get his walk more active before I asked for trot. It worked on the third try (and yes, right on the marker!). I'm so putting that combination in my test.

Oh, time to get back out to the yard. 'Bye!

After dinner—well, it's not my fault if Arabella wants to be moody!

I just can't figure out why she was so mean to me in the lesson and in front of everyone else, too! She was fine at lunch, so maybe she got in a mood because of what happened in this afternoon's dressage workshop. But I don't get *why*—it was nothing really.

We were at the picnic benches again, sketching out rough ideas for our dressage tests with Sally going around helping us. Me and Marie were pacing ours out in front of the barn, as if we were on our ponies, and we got in hysterical giggles 'cos I was whinnying like Lucky does, and Marie was demonstrating around-the-worlds with no pony, which mainly involved twirling while kicking her legs in the air. Then she even asked Sally if we could do them in the comp! Sally said she thought we were crazy girls, but we could if we wanted to. Arabella said we couldn't because it's not an official dressage move, but Sally said, "Well, it's my competition and my rules, so if it makes things even more fun, then why not?"

So maybe Arabella was moody 'cos she didn't get her own way? But still, I don't get why she should care what someone else is doing.

Anyway, I know she was *definitely* in a huff when we went to get ready for our lesson. We had some extra time because Sally was busy in the manège working one-on-one with Emily, the local girl who rides Emerald, Sunnyside's new pony. So Lydia supervised us in the yard, and Marie tried to help me figure out how to fancy Lucky up a bit for the final comp.

We started a mane braid, and can you believe Arabella said, "I don't know why you're bothering. He's so cobby that he's not  going to look fancy, no matter what you do!"

I mean, char-ming! I turned bright red and hugged Lucky's neck. "Yes, he will. He'll look fantastic. Won't you, sweetie?" I said loudly, but Arabella had already wandered away.

When Marie went to help Jojo pick out Sugar's hooves, Arabella came stomping back and said I was *going off* with her! I said, "Marie was helping me. What's wrong with that?" but Arabella got all moody and wouldn't lend me her dandy brush to get the woodchip dust out of Lucky's hind fetlock feather. I don't understand why she acts like she owns me! We're all here to enjoy our ponies and learn dressage and have a good time, so what's the point of making problems when there aren't any?

ᶻ ARGH! ₩

And then in the lesson, the WORST thing happened.

Once we'd warmed up in the manège, Sally said we were going to practice the combination of dressage movements again, but this time in pairs. She explained that this was a good exercise because the more forward-going, confident ponies would give the others a boost. She said Arabella would lead me and Leona would lead Marie, and she was just about to explain what Paula was going to do when Arabella said, "We're not doing the *actual* competition in pairs, are we? Because it's not fair for *them* to affect my score." When she said *them*, she looked at me and Lucky like we were a couple of complete losers.

I was shocked, and I automatically reached down and rubbed Lucky's neck. I felt really embarrassed that she'd said that in front of everyone and also really angry that she could be so

mean to us. Sally was angry, too. "It's only for this lesson," she snapped at Arabella, who just looked sulkily back at her.

"*I'd* like to go with Lauren. I think she's wonderful," said Paula, coming to my rescue.

Sally said, "Yes, all right. And Leona, you can take Arabella over after you've worked with Marie."

Arabella gave me a mean look as if it was

MY fault that she wasn't one of the leaders anymore, when SHE was the one who'd made a fuss. I know she's a perfectionist about the dressage, but that's no reason to be so horrible!

The rest of the lesson went okay, but it was hard to forget about what Arabella had said, and I couldn't concentrate as much as usual. Maybe poor Lucky was upset, too, because he didn't seem himself, either. Between us we were even sloppier about making transitions exactly at the markers, and we didn't get our canter in the AF corner, either, so I had to ride another 20 meter circle in trot and ask again.

But we did finally cheer up when we got to the pairs work, 'cos Lucky really went blazing around after Flame and Paula. I think Flame's showmanship must have inspired him, because he did everything with a lot of style—Sally was right, it *is* easier with someone to copy. She said how good we were, and how much we'd improved already, and I couldn't help grinning. It really boosted my confidence after what

Arabella said. I don't care what she thinks—I'm
so proud of my handsome boy!

In the second half of the lesson, we all went
out of the gate and stood by the fence. Then
one by one, we went back into the manège and
tried out our routines. Lydia came and sat on the
spectators' stand and called out our sequences
for us. It was all very rough and messy, and
we kept stopping when things didn't work and
changing them, with Sally's help, and Lydia wrote
the new things down on our papers.

Lucky tried hard, but he got confused
because some of the things I'd put down were
awkward for him. So my routine changed a lot
in the end as Sally and I found ways to make
it smoother. When Lydia gave me my paper

back, it was very scribbly, so I redrew it up neatly, like this:

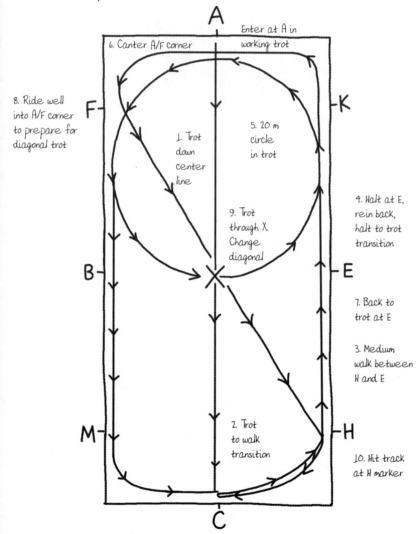

A

Enter at A in working trot

6. Canter A/F corner

8. Ride well into A/F corner to prepare for diagonal trot

F

K

1. Trot down center line

5. 20 m circle in trot

9. Trot through X. Change diagonal

4. Halt at E, rein back, halt to trot transition

B

E

7. Back to trot at E

3. Medium walk between H and E

M

H

2. Trot to walk transition

10. Hit track at H marker

C

11. At C trot down center line, then at A turn right and repeat sequence on other rein

Lauren and Lucky

Oh, I just have to also write that Leona's routine was amazing! She's got these serpentines in it that look really beautiful, and she even tried counter-canter. Because she did it so well, Sally said she could leave it in.

At the end of the lesson, Sally said great job to all of us and also that now is the time to start figuring out our music. Jess's going to help us with that tonight—so hopefully I'll get inspired when I hear a few different things!

In the yard, Arabella kept trying to talk to me, but 'cos I didn't really feel like talking to her, she started going, "What's wrong?"

I kept saying "Nothing" because I couldn't be bothered to go into it—I just wanted to focus on Lucky.

Then she said, "Oh, Lauren, it's not that little thing I said in the lesson, is it?"

I got really angry then because it wasn't a

little thing, it was a great big GIANT thing. I stopped sweeping and leaned on my broom and said, "You say you're my friend, but you're so mean to me ... and to Lucky."

Arabella rolled her eyes. "'Course I'm your friend, silly!" she insisted. "You can't get upset just because I want the best possible chance to win the competition. Since we're friends, you should want me to do well. Don't be so sensitive!"

I WAS ABSOLUTELY FUMING then, and it took me a few seconds to be able to speak. By the time I did, she'd flounced off somewhere else. When she didn't come back, I filled up Gracie's water bucket and finished combing her mane. It wasn't fair for her to suffer just 'cos Arabella was sulking! It's so strange how she doesn't seem interested in taking care of Gracie. She's such a sweet and gorgeous pony—if she was mine, I'd want to spend every single second I could with her!

◡ Lauren and Lucky ◡

So it isn't surprising that I didn't sit with
Arabella at dinner! Instead I went out to the
picnic tables, and luckily Leona called me over
to sit with her and Paula and Marie. We had fun
talking about our freestyle routines, and I did my
best not to look at Arabella, who was sitting with
the younger girls at the next table. When she
walked past us to get seconds from the buffet
in the kitchen, she did this deliberate looking the
other way thing. Leona did this sort of "Ooooh"
raised eyebrows thing at me, and I did it back.

Oh, I wish Arabella would lighten up! I've
been dreaming about my vacation at Pony
Camp for months, ever since Mom said I
could go, and in my imagination there certainly
wasn't a moody girl making things difficult for
me. This is my chance to be one of the girls,
and I want us all to be a big, happy group
hanging out together—I'm not going to let
Arabella spoil everything!

I'm writing this in bed,

after my shower and hot chocolate, waiting for Jess to come and turn the lights off

Last night at this time, we were all chatting away, but tonight Olivia is already fast asleep, and Arabella is reading a magazine. She's turning the pages really loudly to show how much she's ignoring me. Oh, well, I don't care—I wanted time to write in here anyway.

I still haven't had any inspiration about my

music. Leona played me a few songs on her iPod, but none of them was quite right. I also had a look through Olivia's CDs, but nothing stood out. It was really funny helping the others choose, though. We had songs playing through the computer in the game room, and when Paula and Marie picked theirs (which are these two pieces of flamenco music for Paula and this song about being in trouble for Marie), we were figuring out which parts went with which movements.

The younger girls wanted to join in, too, so me, Leona, and Marie gave Polly, Bea, and Jojo piggyback rides around the room, pretending to be the ponies while marking out the dressage steps that Paula was calling out.

Arabella was kind of on her own, but then Olivia started asking her about her routine and stuff, and helping her choose some music from Jess's Popular Classics CD set, so she wasn't completely left out. Anyway, it's not up to me to worry about her—not after how she's been!

Then Jess said we could just about squeeze
in a swim if we were quick, and we all decided
to keep playing ponies in the pool. I gave Jojo
a piggyback ride this time (much easier in
the water!). We pretended the pool was the
manège, and Leona played the part of Sally and
stood in the middle giving us instructions.

Arabella gave Olivia a piggyback ride for a
while, but then she decided she wanted to
do some serious swimming to get fit for the
dressage comp, so Leona took Olivia around
instead. Then we persuaded Jess to be Sally and
do the calling out, even though she thought we
were all completely crazy!

I feel so much better now that I've spent more
time with the other girls. It's a shame that Arabella
was a little left out, but it was her choice.

Oh, Jess's coming up the stairs! Time for
lights out. Good night!

♡ Lauren and Lucky ♡

Wednesday—back at Sunnyside.
We had an amazing day at the
County Show!

There were no yard duties this morning since
we had to head right off in the van, but we did
take some carrots up to the pony field
first, so I got to see my handsome
Lucky before we left.

I sat next to Marie on the way. She let me
listen to one earbud of her iPod, but I didn't
get any inspiration for my dressage music
from it. (I did have an idea later, though!) It
took us about an hour to get to the show,
and Arabella just sat on her own with her
magazines spread out on the seat next to
her, and she didn't talk to anyone the entire
way. But when we got there, she was going,
"Wow!" like everyone else because the show
was much bigger than we'd imagined, with

tons and tons of people everywhere, and a bunch of cute dogs.

When we first got there, we wandered around the booths. There was this one with beautiful silver jewelry on it, and we all tried on different rings and necklaces and stuff, until Jess had to drag us away!

Then Sally called us over to see Barney, the barn owl. He was beautiful and really soft, and we had to be very quiet because he was also shy. Then we looked at the homemade soap booth, where they had all these pretty bars of soap. They looked like candy and smelled delicious—like, there were berry ones and peppermint ones and even chocolate and toffee. I used some of my spending money to buy one

56

for Nana and one for Mom. Smelling the toffee soap made us want some real toffee, so Jess took us over to the fudge stand, and we all bought something to munch on as we went around (I got vanilla).

When the dressage comp started, a bunch of people came over to watch. Sally explained that dressage to music is really popular, even with people who aren't into horses.

The competition was fantastic—the riders were so smart, and the horses were beautifully turned out. They did amazingly tricky movements, like piaffe and passage and even some one-time changes, which are so cool 'cos it looks like the horse is skipping. We all had our faves who we wanted to win—mine was this lady named Felicity Harper on this gorgeous bay, Chickaboom. I liked them because she was a fabulous rider and Chickaboom was very stocky, like Lucky. They did really well, and the crowd loved them (*so there*, Arabella!). And guess what? They came in second—not quite top but pretty awesome!

Afterward, Jess had arranged for us to go into the horsebox area and meet some of the competitors. I was really nervous, and I didn't think I'd know what to say, but then I spotted Felicity sitting on the steps of Chickaboom's trailer, cleaning his tack. I was so excited to tell her how fabulous I thought she was that I completely forgot about feeling shy and just walked over there. I got her autograph, which I'm sticking in here for safekeeping:

> *Good luck in your dressage comp, Lauren and Lucky!*
>
> *Love, Felicity Harper*

◡ Lauren and Lucky ◡

Before I knew it, I was telling her
about how I really want me and
Lucky to do well on
Friday, but how I don't
think we will, not with
him being so laid-back.

She said, "Chicka
can be kind of like that, too, but just be
positive and confident, and I'm sure you'll
inspire Lucky to do his very best. If you play to
his strengths, you'll be fine."

So that got me thinking, and then in the van
on the way back, I got struck with inspiration!
We were all having a singalong of songs from
our fave musicals, and after we'd done that
"oh oh ooooh!" song from *Grease*, Leona
started us all off singing "I'd Do Anything"
from *Oliver*. I suddenly realized that would be
the perfect dressage song for me and Lucky,
because we really *would* do anything for each

other! Lucky is such a scruffy pony! He'll make the perfect Oliver (and it fits his character because he's honest, loyal, and doesn't give up). I'm

scruffy pony

going to be Nancy, and I might even come into the arena twirling an old umbrella, which also shows off the fact that Lucky isn't easily spooked!

When we got back, I told Sally my idea, and she thought it was great! I'm so excited that I've found the perfect song! Jess downloaded it on to the computer for me, and we listened while I helped her set out some lemonade and

cookies (we were thirsty after all that singing!).

Oh, guess what? Sally just came in and said we can go and see our ponies up in the field—'bye!

Wednesday at 9:42 p.m.—
I'm writing this in bed by the
light of my flashlight

The others have gone to sleep.
I did try, but I couldn't stop thinking about
everything that happened this evening. I'm
writing it all down in here because hopefully
then my brain will be able to switch off!

After we'd all had showers, we got into
our pajamas, and I went into the older girls'
room so us four could practice our dressage
tests and help each other learn our sequences
by heart. It was really funny, 'cos we
were doing it like a quiz show,
and when we got something
wrong, Paula was going, "Beep!
Incorrect answer. Good-bye!"

Arabella came and joined in with us when
she'd had her shower. Everything was fine

at first, but when I was in the hot seat, I said
my trot down the center line the wrong way
around, CXA instead of AXC. Paula did the
beep, but then Arabella piped in, shouting,
"Incorrect answer! You are garbage! Please
leave the competition! In fact, don't even
bother entering! You have no chance of
winning on that lazy, scruffy pony anyway!"

I was almost shaking—I just couldn't believe
she'd been *that* horrible to me!

Everyone else was staring at her, but
she just burst into fits of giggles—she obviously
thought she was being *funny*!

Then Leona said to her, "Why don't you
buzz off!" and Paula added, "We didn't even

invite you. You came
barging in, and now
you're ruining things."
Even Marie mumbled,
"Yeah," really quietly.

◡ Lauren and Lucky ◡

Arabella looked surprised at first, and then her eyes filled up with tears, and she ran out of the room.

After that the others complained about her, and I didn't join in at first, but then I thought, *Well, why not, after she's been so mean to me?* So I told them what she'd said about Marie wanting to make Mischief look like a pop star, and about how I've been taking care of Gracie as well as Lucky when she's been too lazy to bother.

Then when we were downstairs having our hot chocolate, the phone rang, and Jess said it was my mom. I stood around the corner on the porch talking to her, 'cos it was too loud in the kitchen, and I told her all about everything I've been up to here at Pony Camp. I even had a quick chat with each of my brothers. I was amazed they wanted to speak to me—they're usually too busy playing outside! Then Mom came back on to say good-bye. When I put

the phone down, I turned around and there
was Arabella, listening in! She went, "I love you,
Mom!"—copying me, but in a mean way.

I was like, "So what? It's my *mom*!"

Arabella made a face and shouted, "*Baby!*"
and then stomped off. I don't get what her
problem is—after all, if she
doesn't like me, why
doesn't she just ignore
me? Why does she have
to trail around after me being
horrible? I don't even know what
she's got to be moody about—she's so lucky;
her life's perfect, and she's got *everything*. It's
not like I even want to be friends with her,
anyway. Not when she's mean and lazy about
taking care of Gracie. It's like she doesn't even
care about her own pony.

Oh, hang on, I can hear something. It sounds
like crying. Let me just go and see....

11:24 p.m.—well, I still can't sleep!

It was Arabella I could hear, crying in the bunk above me. I tried to ignore it, but she sounded so upset I couldn't. I climbed up the ladder and shone my flashlight on her. Her face was buried in the pillow, and she was sobbing her heart out.

"What's wrong?" I whispered. "Are you feeling sick? Should I get Jess?"

Arabella tried to speak but no words came out, just this coughing, choking sound. "No, it's not that," she finally managed to mumble.

I pulled myself up and sat at the end of her bunk. To be honest, I felt really scared, and I didn't know what to do. I was about to get Jess when Arabella started talking. In a whisper she said, "No one likes me."

I thought about fibbing and saying *of course they do*, but I didn't feel like it. Instead I told her the truth. "That's because you're so mean to me."

"Only as a joke," she said weakly.

"Well, *ha ha*," I whispered. "It's pretty mean for a joke, you know. I don't understand you, Arabella. You've got everything. You're so—"

"I know you think I'm lucky, but I'm not," she muttered, then burst into fresh sobs.

"Of course you are," I said. "You've got Gracie." I still felt pretty fed up with her. After all, I'd do anything to have my own pony!

"Gracie hates me," she sniveled.

"What?!" I cried, then clamped my hand over my mouth—I didn't want Jess to hear and come in to tell us to go to sleep. "Is that what you think?" I asked, a lot more quietly. "Is that why you don't bother doing things for her?"

She nodded. "I know she doesn't want me near her, so I try to stay away."

"But how can you think that?" I asked.
"Gracie's so sweet. She's a little high-strung,
maybe, but that's just her being an Arab mare.
She's got a heart of gold."

Arabella sighed. "I've only had her for a
few months, and we just don't seem to get
along," she said then. "At the school stables,
she tried to kick me once when I was braiding
her tail. And she threw me off on a hack. And
she keeps nipping me when I'm trying to tack
her up." Tears ran down her face. "Sometimes
I feel scared to be alone with her," she
admitted.

That really shocked me. I could never be
scared of Lucky or think he hated me. We're
such a team that I just can't imagine it. "Maybe
you should talk to Sally about it in the morning.
She might have some ideas that will help,"
I suggested. Arabella still looked really upset,
so even though I didn't want to, I added, "I'll

come with you if you like."

She wiped her eyes. "Would you really?" she asked. "Even after I've been so horrible to you?"

"Yeah, I guess so," I muttered. "And, hey, what's that all about, anyway? I've never done anything to you." I was trying to make it sound like no big deal, but actually I felt sick, and my heart was pounding. Of course I've had fallouts with my friends and brothers, but no one's ever not liked me before over nothing.

Arabella was quiet for a long time. Then she finally said, "I guess I was jealous because you're so lucky."

"Lucky?" I screeched, and I had to clamp my hand over my mouth again. "Me?" I whispered. "But you've got *everything*!

Freedom, fun, and Gracie. How can you say *I'm lucky?*"

"Your pony adores you, your family's there for you," she said simply. "I hardly ever see my mom and dad. They're not even coming to watch me ride on Friday. And being a boarder sounds fun, but it isn't that great in real life—well, not at my school, anyway. The girls are always gossiping about each other, and you have to get people on your side or you end up alone."

"Is that why you really wanted us to be friends from the start?" I asked. "Because you thought you'd better get someone on your side?"

She nodded. "Yeah. But now I know it's different here. Like you said, there *are* no sides. Well, at least there weren't until I messed everything up. Now no one likes me, and it's just me on my own against everybody else."

"It's not that bad," I began, but I trailed off because, basically, she was absolutely right.

"I'm so sorry, Lauren," she said then. "I'm really ashamed of how I've acted toward you. I'm not surprised the others don't like me, either. But I'm going to change, I really am. Starting right now. I promise I'll make things up to you."

I didn't say anything. I didn't feel like making up with her. And besides, how could I trust that she wouldn't start being mean to me again as soon as we were in front of the others?

"Oh, please, Lauren, give me another chance," she begged, bursting into tears again.

What could I say? She was really upset, and I

did feel a little bit sorry for her after everything she'd told me. So in the end I agreed—we'd forget everything that's happened and make a fresh start, but only if she says she's sorry to Lucky, too!

When I was back down here in my own bunk, staring at nothing and thinking, I started to see that Arabella isn't so lucky after all. Yes, sleepovers at boarding school would be fun, but imagine having one every night and never being able to go home. Sure, having girls around all the time sounds great. But imagine constantly having to worry about who liked you and who didn't—it's not something I ever think about! And yes, my family is annoying sometimes, but they're all coming to see me on Friday, even Dad and Nana. Imagine having parents who'll buy you a pony but are too busy to bother coming to see you ride her! And worst of all, imagine thinking your pony hates you!

Isn't it strange? Sometimes things aren't what they seem at all. And neither are people. Thinking about Arabella's life really makes me appreciate my own. She's right—I *am* the lucky one. I can't wait to give my gorgeous pony a big hug in the morning and tell him how lucky I feel to have him, too!

Actually, now that I've written all this down, I'm feeling tired out myself. I'll just shut my eyes for a minute and

Thursday morning, during our break

I woke Arabella up early, and Jess let us go down and speak to Sally before breakfast. She said she wouldn't allow it usually, but she could tell from our faces that it was important.

We went into the office and Sally was by the sink, filling the kettle. "Hi, girls," she said, "and what can I do for you this early? I haven't even had my coffee yet!"

I looked at Arabella, and Arabella looked at the floor, and Sally looked at both of us and said, "Well?"

Eventually I had to say, "Arabella's scared of Gracie, and we thought you might know what to do."

Sally looked confused.

"She hates me," Arabella said quietly.

She HATES me

73

"Oh, I'm sure that can't be true," said Sally, smiling. She was probably thinking it was just Arabella being difficult again.

"But she does," Arabella insisted. She glanced at me, and I gave her a nod of encouragement. She took a deep breath and told Sally everything about Gracie nipping and kicking and throwing her off.

As Sally listened, her smile turned to a frown. "Well, I haven't noticed anything," she said.

"She doesn't do it when anyone else is around," said Arabella. "Only when I'm in the barn with her, when everyone's busy and distracted. She doesn't want anyone else to see what she's really like."

Sally sighed. "Ponies don't think like that," she said firmly. "It sounds like you've gotten into a vicious cycle. You're nervous when handling her, she picks up on it and gets anxious herself, and then she acts up a bit and you get more nervous. You need to break the cycle. You need to be calm and confident and in control."

"But she—" Arabella began, but Sally interrupted her.

"She doesn't hate you," she insisted. "As I said, ponies don't have those kinds of thoughts."

"Really?" said Arabella.

"I promise," said Sally. "As someone who's had ponies since I was six, spent three years at equestrian college, and five years as an instructor, I think I should know. But you do need to work on building up your relationship. Lauren's got a great partnership going with Lucky. I'm sure she can show you how it's done." She looked at me. "Okay?"

I nodded.

"Thanks, Lauren," Arabella said shyly.

Sally smiled again then and said, "Now, why don't you girls get yourselves in for some breakfast, before Olivia gobbles all the cereal. And don't even think of coming down here this early again!"

"Okay," said Arabella. She already looked much happier.

She went out into the yard, and just as I was following, Sally called me back. "It's very nice of you to help her out," she said. "I've noticed that you two don't exactly get along."

I couldn't help smiling. "Maybe we will now," I said, and headed out.

So after breakfast, we all grabbed some lead ropes and went to catch our ponies. Lydia supervised us in the field, but she wouldn't do it for anyone this time. She said we should have the hang of it by now. After I'd caught Lucky, I noticed that Arabella was still standing in the field with her lead rope, looking uncertain. Tears sprang into her eyes, and she said, "I tried, but whenever I start walking toward her, she just trots away."

"Okay, don't worry," I told her. "Take a deep breath and think positively. Now walk up confidently to her side and clip on the lead rope, as if you expect her to stand still."

Arabella still looked unsure, but she did what I said. And guess what? It worked! She looked so pleased with herself, and she thanked me as we led our ponies out of the field. "See? She's a good girl," I said then. "She just needs to feel that you're confident and in control, that's all."

Gracie was a total sweetie in the yard, too.
I made sure I said a bunch of nice things about
her so that Arabella could see how wonderful
she is. I showed her how to run her hand
down Gracie's side and leg before trying to pick
up her hooves, so that she didn't get startled.
Then when she was trying to sponge her eyes
Gracie gave a loud snort and tossed her head.
Arabella started and jumped backward, but I
just grinned and said, "Don't worry, she's only
saying thank you!" Arabella saw it differently
then and gave Gracie a
big pat, so we're definitely
getting somewhere already!

Oh, and guess what?
Arabella *did* say she was
sorry to Lucky, too! And she made a big fuss
of him, patting his neck and telling him what a
smart boy he was and how great he is going
to be in the dressage comp. He whinnied and

nuzzled her arm, so I know he forgave her—
and I'm sure the half a carrot she gave him
must have helped, too!

Arabella was also a little nervous of
the other dressagers after what happened
yesterday evening, but she took a deep breath
and put on a big smile. And it worked 'cos
soon everyone was happily grooming away in
the yard. Then when she was about to start
using the mane comb on Gracie's body, Paula
pointed to it and went, "Beep!
Uh-uh!" as if we were still playing
quizzes. Everyone laughed, and it
was so funny that Arabella couldn't
help joining in. I grinned at her, and she grinned
back. Maybe she's not so bad after all.

Oh, hang on, here come the others.

In bed–I'm tired out but too
excited to sleep, so I'll just
catch up on my diary

We had our lesson first this morning
so we could practice riding our freestyle tests
to our music. Then during the workshop
time, Sally gave us notes on how we did. We
were all nervous and excited about putting
everything together at last. Lydia called out the
dressage tests for us so we could focus on our
riding. We'll have to have them memorized and
do it alone tomorrow, though!

After a warm-up on each rein and some
general work on balance and impulsion, it was
time to ride the tests. The rest of us went out
into the dirt road to give each rider the whole
manège. We dismounted, held on to our
ponies, and while they munched on grass, we
leaned on the fence to watch.

Gracie started getting a little restless, and Arabella gave me an anxious glance. She was gripping tightly onto the lead rope, so no wonder the poor pony was getting fed up. I told her to relax, let the rope out, and give Gracie some space. She did, and soon Gracie was happily munching on the grass.

"Thanks!" said Arabella. Then she burst out laughing. "*And* for the wonderful grungy green bit I'm going to have to scrub!"

I couldn't help laughing, too, especially when I saw that Lucky had a foaming green mouth to match Gracie's! Ugh!

I was third up after Paula and Marie. I really enjoyed myself— **YUCK!** it felt completely different doing the test to music. Lucky was more alert and quicker off the leg, so I knew he definitely liked the song I'd chosen! Thank goodness Lydia was calling out the test, though, because I would have forgotten all about our halt and rein back at E and gone walking all the way up the long side! I just hope I can get it firmly into my head before tomorrow.

I was really into the rhythm of the music, and I focused on using squeezes on and half halts to get Lucky exactly on the beat. This didn't always work, and it's really tricky to do, but when it did it looked great, so even if I can just get *some* of my routine like that tomorrow, I'll be happy!

After Leona and Arabella had had their turns, we all went back into the manège and cooled down together, and then took our ponies back to the barn and untacked. We were all saying good job to each other and keeping our fingers crossed for good comments from Sally.

Once we'd grabbed drinks and sat down on the benches, Sally gave us her notes. Everyone has things to work on, but me and Lucky seem to have a LOT! They are:

1. Make sure I know the test by heart without it being called.

2. Use the trot down the center line when we first come in to get Lucky listening and awake, by using half halts and squeezing on.

3. Don't worry too much about the lengthened trot strides through X—just normal trot strides are fine. (Phew, 'cos we were having a lot of trouble getting those right!)

4. Keep my head up and look where I'm going—not down Lucky's neck!

5. Keep on track during my canters—don't allow Lucky to cut the corners off.

When Sally had given us all our notes, she said, "So, let's recap. What does the judge expect to see?"

We could just reel off the answer by now because she'd said it so many times, and we all chanted: "Rhythm, impulsion, suppleness, expression, on the bit, straight, good collection, good rider position," and then burst into giggles.

"Okay, good job," she said, rolling her eyes. Then she put us in pairs to work on memorizing our tests, and when I went with Marie, Arabella didn't get moody about it—she just asked if we could be a three. Marie said yes, and it worked out fine.

When we came out after lunch, we were all stressing out about how much practice we still needed to do before the freestyle comp, and all the points we've got to improve on. But

when we got into the yard, Sally really surprised
us by saying, "Actually, what you girls need much
more than practice is to chill out! It's a beautiful
afternoon, and we're going for a hack!"

At first, we were all going, "No, we can't!
We really do need to practice!" But soon we
were having a great time with our ponies,
cantering up stubble fields and trotting down
dirt roads—we even had to go through a river!

At one point, Flame
stumbled over a branch on
the ground and Paula
came tumbling off, and
later on Arabella said
to me that she could see Flame didn't
do it on purpose, and so maybe Gracie
hadn't either when she'd pitched *her* off
that time. She even admitted at dinner that
going on the hack was the best thing we could
have done because she could bond with Gracie

and have fun. (I was amazed because she's usually so obsessed with dressage practice.) In fact, when we were grooming down and caring for our ponies, it was me going, "Come on, hurry up, I'm hungry," because Arabella didn't want to leave Gracie!

Then this evening the fun continued 'cos we had...

A last night dance party!

We all got ready as if we were going to a formal party—Paula did everyone's make-up

with her cool sparkly silver eyeshadow and pink lip gloss, and Bea lent me her silky red flower clip 'cos she was wearing her blue one.

Jess closed the curtains, and Olivia's big

brother Tyler brought his light system into the game room (so I guess brothers are useful sometimes!). We all had a great time dancing around, and after a few songs, Tyler would just suddenly mix in one of our dressage test tunes. When that happened, we would all stand back and let the girl whose song it was pretend to be on her pony and walk through the test. It was so funny, and my jaw was aching from laughing so much, especially at Leona 'cos when her *Black* *Beauty* music came on,

Neigh-hey-hey-hey!

she kept whinnying and pretending her pony was messing around!

I can't wait for the comp tomorrow. I don't think me and Lucky are going to be exactly great, especially not against Paula and Flame, but we're going to try our best and have a lot of fun while we're at it!

Friday—it's the big day, and I'm so excited about the comp!

We're all ready, and we're just waiting for the parents to arrive. I'm really looking forward to seeing my family again—I've missed them a lot. (Okay, I admit it, even my annoying brothers!)

This morning, we had our final lesson (boo-hoo!). We went over the compulsory movements together as a ride, and then we each tried out our tests to music. I was amazed at how much has sunk in simply by us messing around at the dance party last night, and I have definitely fixed points 1, 4, and 5 on my list! We had one turn each, and then Sally said, "That's it, enough, I don't want you to be over-rehearsed." (Like, as if *that* could happen!) Then we got ourselves and our ponies ready and cleaned our tack until it shone.

Now we look like this:

Oh, hey, that's my parents' car!

I'm writing this at home in my own bed–I can't believe Pony Camp is over!

I'm going to pick up exactly where I stopped writing so that I don't leave out anything important!

So, all the parents arrived—well, all except Arabella's. I felt really sad for her when everyone was kissing and hugging each other, so I pulled her over to my mom and Nana, and they gave her a big hug, too, and then all my brothers joined in, and she almost got squished (their hugs are more like being hit by bumper cars)!

It really seemed to cheer her up, and I realized again that I am really, really lucky to have my family, even if it can get loud and chaotic in our house sometimes!

We watched Group A do their gymkhana games and we all cheered really loudly for them. Olivia was amazing and would have won everything, of course, if she hadn't accidentally-on-purpose let Tally gallop off the wrong way in some of the races! Bea and Jojo both won a race and Polly won two, so they were all really happy.

Then it was time for our group to go and get our ponies and mount up for the freestyle dressage—EEEEEEEEEEEEEEEK!

I offered for me and Lucky to go last, because no one else wanted to, and also because Lucky is the most chilled of all the ponies and he was happy to wait, even with all the noise going on.

The crowd absolutely loved the dressage and went crazy clapping after each person's turn. Everyone laughed when Marie's "Uh-Oh, We're in Trouble" song came on because it

suited Mischief perfectly! They rode a great
test, too, although silly Mischief trotted on after
the mark where he should have come back
to walk a couple of times and did an extra
20 meter circle in canter, just because he was
enjoying himself so much!

Paula's Spanish flamenco-themed
test was especially amazing—really
dramatic with a bunch of sudden
halts and changes of pace,
including (can you believe!) halt to *canter*.

Leona was fantastic! Her entrance was
amazing—she launched right into canter in
perfect time with her *Black Beauty* music, and
everyone cheered really loudly! As she prepared
for her counter-canter, we all had our
fingers crossed for her that it
would go okay, and it did! She got it
perfect, and she looked just like the
pros we'd seen at the county show!

◡ Lauren and Lucky ◡

When Arabella's music from the ballet of
Romeo and Juliet came bursting out of the
speakers, all the other girls and my family gave
her a huge cheer to encourage her. I think it
really spurred her on, because she did a great
test. They only had one problem, which was
getting a canter in the AF corner, so they had
to circle around again, but she kept smiling and
didn't get stressed about it, so Gracie followed
her lead and didn't, either.

As Arabella was doing her test, I started
feeling really excited, but nervous, too—I didn't
want to mess up my routine in front of my
whole family. I was getting a little wound up, and
then I remembered the advice that I had given
Arabella only yesterday, which was to chill out,
relax, and have fun. So I took a deep breath and
forced myself to put on a big smile, and soon
I was grinning for real. When it was my and
Lucky's turn to go into the arena, I leaned down

and gave him a big pat and whispered in his ear, "Let's give it our best shot!"

And, well, we definitely did that!

Everyone loved me twirling my umbrella on the way in and gave a big cheer, which made me feel really confident! (I passed it to Lydia before we started the test, of course.)

It was so awesome going around to our music with my amazing pony—just like we were dancing together. We didn't do enough steps of rein back, I forgot how many it was supposed to be, and I went on to the left rein again at A instead of changing and doing everything like a mirror on the right rein. But I corrected it quickly by doing a loop back in the AK corner and kept smiling, so I don't think anyone noticed—well, except Sally and Lydia, of course!

♘ Lauren and Lucky ♘

At the end we got to X and made a square halt (hooray!). Just as the song finished with the words "I'd do anything, anything for you," Lucky snorted and shook his head like he was agreeing, and everyone went "Ahhh!" 'cos he looked so cute.

I was so proud of him, of us, that I felt like I might burst. If it had been a comp for the most gorgeous pony, we definitely would have won! We didn't, of course—Sally said it was a really close call between Paula and Leona, but in the end she awarded Leona first prize and Paula second. Something totally amazing did happen, though—Lucky and I came in third (and got a beautiful green rosette)! There wasn't a fourth or fifth place, but Marie and Arabella got these pretty pink rosettes, too, for taking part.

I thought Arabella might be a little moody with me for finishing ahead of her, but in fact she gave me a big hug and said great job (and made a fuss of Lucky, too).

When I said great job back to her, she just shrugged. "Not really that great," she said. "We couldn't get our canter, and I lost the rhythm of the music a couple of times, and—"

"But you worked together and you both looked comfortable and relaxed, and anyone could tell Gracie was really listening to you," I pointed out. "Those things are much more important than getting it technically perfect."

"Thanks," she said. "And thanks for all your help with Gracie. We couldn't have done any of it without you. You'd make a great instructor, you know."

I couldn't help beaming when she said that. I imagined myself in Sally's shoes in a few years'

time. I'd love that more than anything in the world. Well, maybe if I work hard on my riding, and help out a lot at my local stables, and read up on pony care, who knows? Maybe I'll be able to get into equestrian college, too!

Of course, my dad recorded everything like he always does, and he said he'll burn a copy of it for Arabella so she can show her parents when she visits them. She looked a little upset when he mentioned them, but Mom gave her another hug and said she bet they were really wishing they could be here with us at Pony Camp, and how she was sure they were fed up with being stuck at work far away in another country.

I hadn't thought of it like that before, and maybe Arabella hadn't, either, because she seemed to cheer up even more then.

When it was time to go home, I spent a long time in the barn with Lucky, making sure he had enough water and checking his hooves for stones and just giving him a ton of hugs and telling him how much I love him. Plus, I said I'll look at his picture every day and never forget him, and I'll try to persuade Mom to let me come back next year. He nuzzled into my shoulder and snorted gently, so I know he felt just like I did.

All the other girls were the same—none of us wanted to leave our ponies. We were all taking group pics of us with our ponies, and Polly even asked me to take one of her mucking out poop to show her brother she really did do it 'cos he didn't believe she would!

Finally, it was really, absolutely, definitely time to go (in Sally's words), so we all took a few final photos with her and Lydia and Jess and Olivia, and then we started heading off to our cars.

Arabella was staying until we'd all gone, because Jess was driving her back to her boarding school later on with Gracie in the

horse box, then she's going to Boulder,
Colorado, to do outdoor activities. She gave
me another big hug, and we kept saying
good-bye and then starting to talk again until
Mom had to pretty much order me into the
car! We're going to write to each other, and
Mom says maybe she can come and
stay at the end of the vacation. I can't
believe we've ended up being such
good friends after everything that's
happened!

I'm just so lucky that I went to Pony Camp
and that I got Lucky the pony, and I'm also so
lucky to have such a caring family.

Oh, gotta go—Mom's calling me down to
set the table for dinner. Ugh! I think I'll go and
ask her why my brothers can't help, and I'll
keep how lucky I feel to myself!

Lauren 🍀

PONY CAMP
diaries

Learn all about
the world of ponies!

Glossary

Bending—directing the horse to ride correctly around a curve

Bit—the piece of metal that goes inside the horse's mouth. Part of the bridle.

Chase Me Charlie—a show jumping game where the jumps get higher and higher

Currycomb—a comb with rows of metal teeth used to clean (to curry) a pony's coat

Dandy brush—a brush with hard bristles that removes the dirt, hair, and any other debris stirred up by the currycomb

Frog—the triangular soft part on the underside of the horse's hoof. It's very important to clean around it with a hoof pick.

Girth—the band attached to the saddle and buckled around the horse's barrel to keep the saddle in place

Grooming—the daily cleaning and caring for the pony to keep them healthy and make them beautiful for competitions. A full grooming includes brushing your pony's coat, mane, and tail and picking out the hooves.

Gymkhana—a fun event full of races and other competitions

Hands—a way to measure the height of a horse

ೕ Glossary ೕ

Mane—the long hair on the back of a horse's neck. Perfect for braiding!

Manège—an enclosed training area for horses and their riders

Numnah—a piece of material that lies under the saddle and stops it from rubbing against the horse's back

Paces—a pony has four main paces, each made up of an evenly repeated sequence of steps. From slowest to quickest, these are the walk, trot, canter, and gallop.

Plodder—a slow, reliable horse

Pommel—the raised part at the front of the saddle

Pony—a horse under 14.2 hands in height

Rosette—a rose-shaped decoration with ribbons awarded as a prize! Usually, a certain color matches where you are placed during the competition.

Stirrups—foot supports attached to the sides of a horse's saddle

Tack—the main pieces of the pony's equipment, including the saddle and bridle. Tacking up a horse means getting them ready for riding.

Pony Colors

*Ponies come in many different **colors**. These are some of the most common!*

Bay—Bay ponies have rich brown bodies and black manes, tails, and legs.

Black—A true black pony will have no brown hairs, and the black can be so pure that it looks a bit blue!

Chestnut—Chestnut ponies have reddish-brown coats that vary from light to dark red with no black points.

Dun—A dun pony has a sandy-colored body, with a black mane, tail, and legs.

Gray—Gray ponies come in a range of color varieties, including dapple gray, steel gray, and rose gray. They all have black skin with white, gray, or black hair on top.

Palomino—Palominos have a sandy-colored body with a white or cream mane and tail. Their coats can range from pale yellow to bright gold!

Piebald—Piebald ponies have black-and-white patches—like a Fresian cow!

Skewbald—Skewbald ponies have patches of white and brown.

Pony Markings

*As well as the main body color, many ponies also have white **markings** on their faces and legs!*

On the legs:

Socks—run up above the fetlock but lower than the knee. The fetlock is the joint several inches above the hoof.

Stockings—extend to at least the bottom of the horse's knee, sometimes higher

On the face:

Blaze—a wide, straight stripe down the face from in between the eyes to the muzzle
Snip—a white marking on the pony's muzzle, between the nostrils
Star—a white marking between the eyes
Stripe—the same as a blaze but narrower
White/bald face—a very wide blaze that goes out past the eyes, making most of the pony's face look white!

Fan-tack-stic Cleaning Tips!

*Get your **tack** shining in no time with these top tips!*

- Clean your tack after every use, if you can. Otherwise, make sure you at least rinse the bit under running water and wash off any mud or sweat from your girth after each ride.

- The main things you will need are:
  - bars of saddle soap
  - a soft cloth
  - a sponge
  - a bottle of leather conditioner

- As you clean your bit, check that it has no sharp edges and isn't too worn.

- Use a bridle hook or saddle horse to hold your bridle and saddle as you clean them. If you don't have a saddle horse, you can hang a blanket over a gate to put the saddle on. Avoid hanging your bridle on a single hook or nail because the leather might crack!

- Make sure you look carefully at the bridle before undoing it so that you know how to put it back together!
- Use the conditioner to polish the leather of the bridle and saddle and make them sparkle!
- Check under your numnah before you clean it. If the dirt isn't evenly spread on both sides, you might not be sitting straight as you ride.
- Polish your metalwork occasionally. Cover the leather parts around it with a cloth and only polish the rings—not the mouthpiece, because that would taste horrible!

Dazzle in Dressage!

Find out how to dazzle in dressage competitions with this fun quiz!

1. "Dressage" means "training" in:
   a.   Elvish
   b.   French
   c.   Latin

2. The beginner level of dressage tests is called:
   a.   First
   b.   Novice
   c.   Introductory

3. You should only bandage your pony's legs in dressage for:
   a.   Training
   b.   Competitions
   c.   Both training and competitions

4. A transition is:
   a.   A change from one marker to another
   b.   A change in direction
   c.   A change from one pace to another

5. During a pirouette, the parts of your pony that need to stay in the same place are:
 a. The hind legs
 b. The front legs
 c. All the pony's legs

6. The correct terms to describe making your pony's steps shorter and longer are:
 a. Shortening and lengthening
 b. Contraction and expansion
 c. Collection and extension

7. The highest level of dressage competitions is:

 a. Advanced
 b. Grand Prix
 c. Championship

8. Which of the following is NOT a dressage movement?
 a. Counter-canter
 b. Flying Charges
 c. Flying Scotsman

❧ Beautiful Braids! ❧

Follow this step-by-step guide to give your pony a perfect tail braid!

1. Start at the very top of the tail and take two thin bunches of hair from either side, braiding them into a strand in the center.

2. Continue to pull in bunches from either side and braid down the center of the tail.

3. Keep braiding like this, making sure you're pulling the hair tightly to keep the braid from unraveling!

4. When you reach the end of the dock—where the bone ends—stop taking in bunches from the side but keep braiding downward until you run out of hair.

5. Fasten with a braid band!

Gymkhana Ready!

Get your pony looking spectacular for the gymkhana with these grooming ideas!

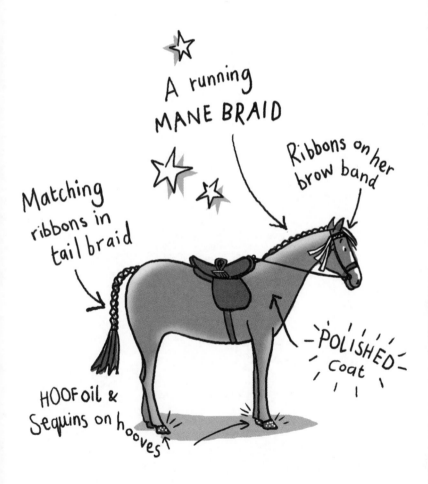

A running MANE BRAID

Ribbons on her brow band

Matching ribbons in tail braid

POLISHED Coat

HOOF oil & Sequins on hooves

Turn the page for a sneak peek
at another story in the series!

PONY
CAMP
diaries

Jessica and
Jewel

by Kelly
McKain

Illustrated
by Mandy
Stanley

Monday—a little past 9 a.m.
I've just arrived here at Pony Camp!

My little sister Tegan and I are the first ones here because Mom had an early meeting and she needed to drop us off beforehand. Jess (the nice lady who runs Pony Camp) is still busy figuring out all the sleeping arrangements upstairs, so we're sitting at the kitchen table at the moment. She gave us some juice and drawing stuff to keep us busy, and these cool Pony Camp Diaries, one each, which is what I'm writing in right now. Tegan is drawing a fairy with pink wings, but also skinny jeans like mine and furry boots.

I'm so excited about Pony Camp! I can't wait to find out which pony I'm getting, and spending a whole week riding will be fantastic!

I usually go to the stables on Saturday mornings (Tegan comes, too), and I'm not great or anything, but I know the basics. I can walk, trot, and canter and do some of the trickier transitions like halt to trot (well, sometimes, if I'm on Molly!). I've even tried some jumping on Gingersnap, including a few combinations. My instructor Jane tries to switch us each week so we get a lot of experience on different ponies. That's great, but it'll be so exciting to have the same pony all this week, as if he (or she!) is actually mine!

Oh, it's going to be so COOL! —I'll have my own pony, and be sharing a room with girls my own age! At home I have to share with Tegan, which means I'm always tripping over her dolls, and she's always taking my glitter eyeshadow and wasting TONS! And it means NO noise after 7:30 p.m. when she goes to bed—so no video games or TV or music. I'm allowed my bedside lamp on to read, but I even have to turn the pages of my book quietly!

I'm super into boarding school books at the moment, and I'm extra excited because this week will be just like boarding school, but even better 'cos we'll have ponies. I've bought tons of stuff for a midnight snack and I've been saving up a few really juicy secrets to tell when we do our whispering in the middle of the night.

And I chose to come especially this week because there's going to be a trail ride and campout! I've always been into cowboys and western stuff, so going on a real trail ride is a dream come true! Getting to trek through miles and miles of open country, and camping out under the stars, and having hot dogs and beans, and singing around the fire will be so exciting!

Tegan isn't bothered about the trail ride, or even about ponies that much, but of course as soon as I showed Mom the brochure for Pony Camp,  my sister wanted to come, too. Mom and Dad were definitely agreeable to that, because if we both went, it meant they could have a break away on their own, so they're off to New York City tomorrow. I said, "What about *me* having a vacation by myself without Tegan?"

Mom laughed and replied, "Well, Dad and I haven't had a vacation by ourselves since before you were born, so I figure we get priority, don't you, Jess? Anyway, think about your sister. She'd much rather be with you and a lot of other girls than just us two."

Mom doesn't understand and, well, it is hard to explain. It's not like I *mind* T being here, but it's … well, I kind of just want to be me, Jess, and do my own thing, without having to worry about taking care of her for a change. I mean, of course I like doing things with her, she's my little sister, but she's 7 and I'm 10 and a half, so it's not exactly as though we enjoy the same things. She always wants me to play these made-up games with her, like school or doctor, and sometimes they go on for hours. Mom and Dad run a mail order business together, and they're usually in their office (i.e., the spare room), and they're always saying "in a minute" and "I just need to finish this," so I'm left doing stuff with Tegan a lot of the time.

Oh, well—we're both here now and that's that, so there's no point complaining about it. Hopefully there'll be some younger girls she can make friends with.

I can't wait for everyone else to get here so Pony Camp can really get started! Then I'll have TONS to write about!

I'm quickly writing this while everyone's getting their stuff unpacked

Can you believe it? Tegan and I have been put in a room together because we're sisters. All my sleepover plans are completely ruined, and it's going to be just like it is at home (i.e., BORING!).

z ARGH! w

When everyone started arriving, Jess showed us all upstairs, and there were these three really awesome older girls and three younger, and I thought, oh, good, two rooms of four, so I can go in with the older ones. But then it turned out there are actually three rooms and that I'm sharing with Tegan.

I really wanted to ask if I could go in with the older girls instead, but I didn't want to seem like a complainer, and anyway there are no spare beds in there, so I tried to act like

I didn't mind. In addition to our bunk bed, there's a single bed by the window. Jess said it was her daughter Olivia's, and I cheered up 'cos I thought, *Well at least we'll be sharing with someone else.* But then she said Olivia's away this week staying with her aunt, so it really is only going to be me and Tegan. All my imaginings about midnight snacks and whispering girly secrets went poof out of my head and I just stood there feeling glum, until Tegan brought me back to reality by making a big deal about having the top bunk.

Unpacking my stuff on the bottom bunk did cheer me up a bit, though. I kept thinking, *Wow, I'm actually here at Pony Camp—and staying for a whole week!* I don't suppose sharing with T will be all that bad. Maybe when she goes to sleep, I'll be able to sneak into the older girls' room for midnight snacks so I don't completely miss out. I'm definitely not going to let it stop me from enjoying this week, anyway. After all, I can't wait to meet my pony, and there's the trail ride to look forward to, and all the lessons and helping out in the yard (and mucking out—ugh—hee-hee!).

Oh, we're being called downstairs now—time to go and meet the other girls, and find out which pony I'm getting!

If you love animals, check out these series, too!

Pet Rescue Adventures

The Perfect Kitten
by HOLLY WEBB

The Seaside Puppy
by HOLLY WEBB

The Unwanted Puppy
by HOLLY WEBB

The Kidnapped Kitten
by HOLLY WEBB

ANIMAL RESCUE CENTER

ANIMAL RESCUE CENTER

The Abandoned Hamster

by TINA NOLAN

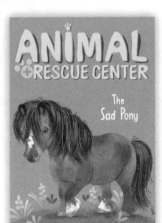

ANIMAL RESCUE CENTER

The Sad Pony

by TINA NOLAN

ANIMAL RESCUE CENTER

The Homeless Foal

by TINA NOLAN

ANIMAL RESCUE CENTER

The Porch Puppy

by TINA NOLAN

Kelly McKain

Kelly McKain is a best-selling children's and YA author with more than 50 books published in more than 20 languages. She lives in the beautiful Surrey Heath area of the UK with her family and loves horses, dancing, yoga, singing, walking, and being in nature. She came up with the idea for the Pony Camp Diaries while she was helping young riders at a summer camp, just like the one at Sunnyside Stables! She enjoys hanging out at the Holistic Horse and Pony Center, where she plays with and rides cute Smartie and practices her natural horsemanship skills with the Quantum Savvy group. Her dream is to do some bareback, bridleless jumping like New Zealand Free Riding ace Alycia Burton, but she has a ways to go yet!